Every Mom Is Special

Published in Nashville, Tennessee, by Oliver-Nelson Books, a division of Thomas Nelson, Inc., Publishers, and distributed in Canada by Word Communications, Ltd., Richmond, British Columbia.

The Bible version used in this publication is the Contemporary English Version. Copyright © 1991, American Bible Society.

Library of Congress Cataloging - in - Publication Data

Jenks, Graham.
    Every mom is special / written by Graham Jenks : illustrated by Priscilla Burris.
       p.   cm.
Summary: All of God's creatures have mothers who take care of them and love them in special ways.
    ISBN 0-7852-8215-7 (hardcover)
    [1. Mothers —Fiction. 2. Christian life—Fiction.] I. Burris, Priscilla, ill. II. Title.
PZ7.J425He   1994
[E]—dc20   93-35481
                                                        CIP
                                                         AC

Printed in the United States of America.

1 2 3 4 5 6 — 99 98 97 96 95 94

Every Mom Is Special

Written by
Graham Jenks

Illustrated by
Priscilla Burris

OLIVER
NELSON

THOMAS NELSON PUBLISHERS
Nashville

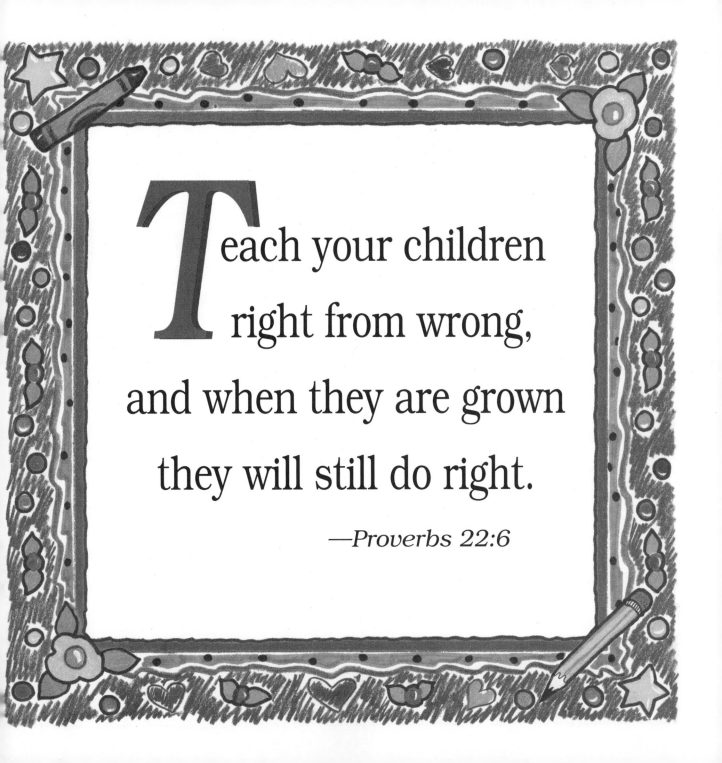

Teach your children right from wrong, and when they are grown they will still do right.

—*Proverbs 22:6*

Animals have moms just like we do. God planned it that way.

Our moms take good care of us.

There is so much to learn when we are small.
So God put moms everywhere to help us.

Learning new things is fun when we do it with
our moms.

They helped us take our first steps.

They were excited when they
heard our first words.

Moms know that
when we are young,
we need to frolic
and play.

They do not want us
to eat junk food.

They feed us good things so we will grow up strong and healthy.

Keeping neat and clean is important to our moms.

They always want us to look our best.

Moms tell their friends how wonderful we are.

They show us how to cross the street safely.

They teach us what to do if we get lost.

If our feelings get hurt, moms give us a kiss and a hug.

When things go wrong, moms listen to us.
Then we talk to God about it.

Sometimes moms lose their patience
if we act wild or get too noisy.

Afterward we say we are sorry. We hug our moms. And like God, our moms forgive us and love us just as we are. We feel better now.

When families travel, moms take along fun things to do. They do not want us to get bored. But still we ask, "Are we there yet?"

Moms help us get ready for the future.

Then when we grow up, we will be able to take care of ourselves.

When we get crabby, moms say, "No one likes to be around a grouch."

When we act stubborn, they tell us
we cannot always have our way.

Moms teach us that things go better
when we work together.

We will always be their children,
even when we are very old.

Moms here

Moms there

Moms, moms everywhere

Sharing God's love

and showing God's care.